"...come on." Dee Dee headed for the den door.

"Wait a minute," I said. "Where are we going?"

"To the yacht club," she said.

"What about my roast beef?" I asked.

"I promise I'll give it to you when we come back," she said

"That's not fair," I said.

"But the desk at the yacht club closes at six," Dee Dee said.

"So, *you* go," I said.

"You know Mom and Dad don't like me to go outside in the evening alone," Dee Dee said.

"But I've already had two walks today," I said. "That exceeds my daily quota."

Dee Dee put her hands on her hips and gave me an impatient look.

"For Pete's sake, Wordsworth. This is important."

"To whom?" I asked.

"Oh, all right," Dee Dee said. "Come with me to the yacht club and you'll get *two* slices of roast beef when we get back."

"Now you're talking," I said

Wordsworth and the Roast Beef Romance

by Todd Strasser

HarperPaperbacks
A Division of HarperCollins*Publishers*

This is a work of fiction. The characters, incidents, and dialogues are products of the author's imagination and are not to be construed as real. Any resemblance to actual events or persons, living or dead, is entirely coincidental.

HarperPaperbacks *A Division of* HarperCollins*Publishers*
10 East 53rd Street, New York, N.Y. 10022

Cover and interior illustrations by Leif Peng
Cover and interior art ©1995 Creative Media Applications, Inc.

First HarperPaperbacks printing: August 1995

Printed in the United States of America

HarperPaperbacks and colophon are trademarks of HarperCollins*Publishers*

❖ 10 9 8 7 6 5 4 3 2 1

To Eli, Emma, and Fluffy Weasel Fuchsberg

Wordsworth and the Roast Beef Romance

One

――∞∞∞――

"What's wrong with Roy?" Dee Dee
Chandler asked me.

I, Maxwell Short Wordsworth the Sixth, was wriggling on my back on the kitchen floor, trying to scratch an itch.

"Wordsworth?" Dee Dee said. "I asked if you know what's wrong with Roy."

Dee Dee is ten years old and has blond hair and freckles. She's my best friend. She was sitting at the kitchen table, drawing pictures of fish on a white sheet of paper. It was around nine o'clock at night.

"I don't know," I said. I was still wriggling. The itch was right in the middle of my back. I couldn't reach it with my paw. It was driving me crazy!

"He's acting weird," Dee Dee said. Her parents had gone out, and so had her older sister, Janine. That meant only Dee Dee and Roy were home. Roy was baby-sitting Dee Dee that night. We could see him on

1

the back deck outside the kitchen. He was sitting in a white plastic chair. The sliding glass door between the kitchen and the deck was closed, so Dee Dee could talk to me without worrying that her brother might hear us. Dee Dee and I don't want anyone to know I can talk. That's because I'm a basset hound.

"Roy always acts weird," I said. "There's nothing new about that."

"Something is different, Wordsworth," Dee Dee said. "He's acting weirder than usual."

Roy is fourteen. He spends most of his time in his room watching TV and lifting weights. Now that it's summer, he also goes to the village pool almost every day to swim.

That itch still wouldn't go away. I rolled over onto my stomach.

"Could you do me a huge favor?" I asked.

"Sure, Wordsworth." Dee Dee smiled. "Where's it itch?"

"About halfway down my back," I said. "Dead center."

She reached down and started to scratch my back. She's a good soul.

"Oh, yeah!" I moaned. "Now over to the right a little. Oh, yeah! Oh, yeah! That's it . . . *that's it*!"

It felt great. Dee Dee has magic fingers. Once she'd taken care of my itch, I could focus more on Roy.

"Why do you think he's acting weirder than usual?" I asked, stretching out.

"Look." Dee Dee pointed out the sliding glass kitchen door. Roy was staring up at the moon. It was large and round and glowing. From deep inside me came a strong desire to howl. I forced it back down. It embarrasses me when I act like an animal.

"He's allowed to stare at the moon," I said.

"For an hour?" Dee Dee asked.

"Maybe he's turning into Wolfman," I said. "Or, in Roy's case, Wolfboy."

"I think something's wrong," Dee Dee said. "I'm worried about him."

"If you really think something's wrong, why don't you ask him?"

"Okay, I will." Dee Dee got up and slid open the kitchen door. She went out onto the deck. I got on my feet and followed, just in case Roy was growing fur on the backs of his hands.

It was warm and humid outside. The air smelled like flowers.

"Roy?" Dee Dee said.

"Hmmm?" Roy kept staring at the moon.

"Is there something wrong?" Dee Dee asked.

Roy didn't answer. I decided to lie down on the deck. A small moth fluttered by. I thought about eating it. Then I remembered I'd eaten a moth once. It tasted sort of chalky.

"I said, is there something wrong?" Dee Dee asked again.

"Why do you ask?" Roy said.

"You've been staring at the moon for an hour."

For the first time in a hour, Roy turned. He hadn't grown fur on his face and he didn't have fangs. I guess he wasn't turning into Wolfboy after all.

"Dee Dee, if you were a girl—" Roy began to say.

"I *am* a girl," Dee Dee reminded him.

"Yeah, but if you were a *real* girl," Roy said.

"I *am* a real girl," Dee Dee said.

"I meant older," Roy said. "What would make you like a boy?"

Dee Dee thought for a second and then said, "Nothing."

Roy made a face. "I said, if you were *older*."

"Janine's older and she doesn't like boys," Dee Dee said.

"Janine doesn't *have* to like boys," said Roy. "They all like her."

A firefly flew past my nose. I'd once eaten one of those too. It tasted bitter.

"I'm sorry, Roy, I don't think I can help you with this," Dee Dee said.

"Right." Roy got up and went into the kitchen.

"Hey, where are you going?" Dee Dee asked.

"Up to my room," he said.

"But you're supposed to baby-sit me," Dee Dee said.

Roy stopped and looked back at her. "Keep the doors locked, don't play with matches, and if you get hungry, look in the refrigerator."

Then he turned and went upstairs.

4

Two

"Come on, Wordsworth," Dee Dee said.
She and I went into the den. I lay down on the rug.
Dee Dee sat on the couch.

"So what do you want to do?" she asked.

"Sleep," I said with a yawn.

"Please don't," Dee Dee said. "I need someone to
play with."

The phone started to ring.

"Aren't you going to answer it?" I asked.

"There's no point," Dee Dee said. "It's just some
guy calling for Janine."

"How do you know?" I asked.

"Listen."

The phone machine clicked on. The message said,
"Hello, you've reached the Chandler residence. Please
leave a message after the beep."

The machine beeped, and a boy started to talk.
"Uh, hi, this is a message for Janine. Janine, it's Rick

5

Berger. I met you at the yacht club yesterday, remember? Anyway, I was wondering if you were free on Saturday night."

"See?" Dee Dee said. "It's *always* for Janine. So, want to do a jigsaw puzzle?"

"Oh, okay," I said. I really wasn't in the mood for a jigsaw puzzle, but for Dee Dee's sake I'd do it.

Dee Dee spilled the pieces of the puzzle on the floor and started to put them together. She did jigsaw puzzles by putting together all the pieces with the same colors.

"I've never seen anyone do a jigsaw puzzle like that," I said.

"How do *you* do them, smarty-pants?" Dee Dee asked.

"The logical way. I start with the edge and work my way in."

"Wait a minute," Dee Dee said. "I've never even seen you do a jigsaw puzzle."

"They weren't made for creatures with paws," I said.

The front door opened and Janine came in. Janine is sixteen years old. She is tall and blond and beautiful.

"A lot of boys called," Dee Dee said. "I let the phone machine take all the calls. Where were you?"

"Brooke and I were getting her sailboat ready for Race Week," Janine said. "It starts tomorrow. We're racing in the four-twenty class this year."

Each year the yacht club has Race Week. Kids from

all over Bell Island Sound come to race in it. Janine sat down on the couch and brushed her blond hair out of her eyes with her hand.

"Wow, I'm tired," she said.

The tip of my tail began to itch. I *hated* that! Now I had to curl around in a circle and try to chew my tail. It always invites mean comments from humans.

"What's with that dog?" Janine asked.

"His tail probably itches," Dee Dee said. She reached for my tail and held it until I could grab it with my teeth. Good old Dee Dee!

"You're not home alone, are you?" Janine asked.

"Roy's upstairs," Dee Dee said.

"Watching TV and lifting weights?"

"Probably," Dee Dee said. "But a little while ago he sat on the back deck and stared at the moon for an hour."

Janine nodded.

"Don't you think that's strange?" Dee Dee asked.

"Not really," her older sister said.

"He's never done that before," Dee Dee said. "How can you say it's not strange?"

"Well, it is strange, but not for Roy," said Janine.

"Why?"

"Because he's fourteen and he needs a girlfriend."

"When boys look at the moon it means they need a girlfriend?" Dee Dee scowled.

"If they're not using a telescope," Janine said. "Haven't you noticed the way he's been acting lately?

He's always moping around the house. He spends hours in the bathroom combing his hair in different ways. He's even started to use deodorant."

"I thought that was because he smelled," Dee Dee said, wrinkling her nose.

"Boys don't care if they smell unless girls are involved," Janine said with great authority.

"So why doesn't he get a girlfriend?" Dee Dee asked.

"He doesn't know how," Janine said. She yawned. Obviously the subject bored her.

By then I had finished chewing my tail. The itch had gone away. I put my head in Dee Dee's lap and she scratched me behind the ears. There is nothing better in life than having a good human.

"Can't we help him?" Dee Dee asked.

Janine shook her head. "We can't help him because he'll never admit to us that he needs a girlfriend. Not unless he gets *really* desperate."

"But you must know some girls his age," Dee Dee said. "Couldn't you ask them if they'd like to be Roy's girlfriend?"

"No way," said Janine. "You can't go around asking girls to be your brother's girlfriend."

"Why not?"

"Because every girl you ask is going to wonder why Roy doesn't get a girlfriend by himself," Janine said. "They're going to assume he's a dork. Which, in Roy's case, isn't far from the truth."

Wordsworth and the Roast Beef Romance

"But then he'll never find a girlfriend," Dee Dee said.

"That's life." Janine yawned and stood up. "I'm going to bed. See you in the morning."

Janine left the den. Dee Dee held my head in her hands and looked into my eyes.

"I think we should try to help Roy," she said.

"How?" I asked.

"I don't know," she said. "But I'll try to think of something."

Three

The next afternoon, Dee Dee took me
for a walk in Soundview Manor Park. Race Week had
begun, and Bell Island Sound was filled with sailboats
competing against one another. Each class of boat was
having its own race. The boats in each class were tightly
grouped together as they vied to see who was the fastest.

Down on the rocks near the water's edge, Dee
Dee's mom, Flora, had set up her easel and was painting a picture of the sailboats. Flora was wearing a
white dress and a white sun hat. Her long blond hair
hung down her back.

Dee Dee and I found some shade under a tree and
lay down next to each other on the grass. She put her
arm around my neck and moved her face close to mine
so we could talk and not be overheard.

"Isn't this nice?" she whispered.

I looked around to make sure no other humans
could hear us. Then I said, "It's okay."

Wordsworth and the Roast Beef Romance

"But you'd rather be sailing, right?" she guessed.

"Yes." Sailing is the one sport I enjoy. I love being out on the water with the wind in the sails, the sea spray in my face, and my ears flapping in the breeze. Of course, the part I like best is the large picnic basket filled with fried chicken and other goodies that Flora always packs. There is nothing like being on the water to create an appetite.

The other great thing about sailing is that I don't have to do anything except lie on the deck. The Chandlers even had a special basset hound–shaped life preserver made just in case I fall overboard.

"Ahoy there!" someone shouted.

Dee Dee and I looked up and saw a small sailboat tacking close to shore. A tall, white-haired man was sailing on it and he was waving at Flora and us.

"It's Dad!" Dee Dee cried, and jumped up. She ran down to the rocks and waved back. "Hi, Dad. Where'd you get the boat?"

"I just bought it," Leyland Chandler said.

Flora left her painting and joined us. "But we already have a sailboat, dear."

"This one is for a new invention I'm working on," Leyland said as he sailed past. The boat was much smaller than their other sailboat, and it looked very old. Bits of white paint flaked off its wooden sides, and the sail had patches sewn on it.

We watched as Leyland sailed back into the sound. Then Flora returned to her painting. I was hoping that

we'd go back to the shade and lie down again, but Dee Dee clipped the leash to my collar.

"We'd better get going," she whispered.

"But I was just getting comfortable," I said.

"You never have trouble getting comfortable at home," Dee Dee said.

We started along a path that led out of the park. Ahead, a group of girls was coming toward us. They looked older than Dee Dee, but younger than Janine. None of them looked familiar. I assumed they were all visiting for Race Week.

"Oh, look at that dog!" one of them said as they came closer.

"He's so adorable!" gasped another.

The next thing I knew, they all were crowding around Dee Dee and me.

"Does he bite?"

"Not unless you're a roast beef sandwich," Dee Dee said.

"Can we pet him?" one of the girls asked.

"Sure," Dee Dee said.

Half a dozen hands began to pet and scratch me. I quickly lay down and rolled onto my back so they could scratch my tummy. This was great!

"He's a basset hound, isn't he?" one of the girls asked.

"Yup," Dee Dee said.

"Isn't he huge?"

"He's eighty-five pounds," Dee Dee said. She

sounded proud. I was surprised because usually she wants me to lose weight.

After a while the girls got tired of scratching me and left. I stood up and we started walking home again.

"Gee, I never knew you were so popular," Dee Dee teased me.

"That's me," I replied. "Mr. Popularity!"

Suddenly Dee Dee stopped and stared down at me. "I've got it, Wordsworth!"

"Got what?"

"The perfect way for us to help Roy find a girl-friend!"

Four

That evening Dee Dee came into the kitchen to make herself and me dinner. I had just awakened from a long afternoon nap. Dinner at the Chandlers' is very strange. Everyone makes whatever they want for themselves. The only person who cooks for anyone else is Dee Dee. She always makes me a lamb chop.

"Do you know who is going to find Roy a girl-friend?" Dee Dee asked as she broiled my lamb chop in the oven.

"The Dial-a-Date Hotline?" I yawned.

"No," said Dee Dee. "You."

"Me?" I sat up. "How?"

"Remember what happened when we walked home from the park today?" she asked.

"I stopped to sniff about twenty trees," I said.

"What else?"

"I saw a squirrel but it was too far away to chase."

15

"And what else?" Dee Dee asked.

"Hmmm." I had to think. "Oh, I know. All those girls stopped to pet me."

"Exactly," Dee Dee said. "Now what do you think would have happened if Roy had been walking you?"

"He never would have let me stop to sniff the trees," I said. Roy is the worst dog walker in the world. On those rare occasions when Dee Dee can't walk me, the Chandlers ask Roy to do it. Roy always hurries around the block. He never lets me stop to sniff anything.

"No, no, silly," Dee Dee said. "Roy would have met all those girls."

"So?"

"So maybe one of them would want to be his girl-friend."

That's when I started to figure out what she had in mind. "Wait a minute," I said. "You're not going to have Roy walk me."

"Don't you want him to find a girlfriend?" Dee Dee asked.

"To tell you the truth, it's not something I really care about one way or the other," I said.

"Don't you want him to be happy?" Dee Dee asked.

"But he never lets me stop to sniff anything," I said.

"I'll talk to him about that," Dee Dee said.

"I still don't like it," I said. "I want *you* to walk me."

"I will," Dee Dee said. "Once Roy has a girlfriend."

"Why is it so important for Roy to have a girl-friend?" I asked.

"Because it just is," Dee Dee said. "People in this town think we're strange already. If Roy doesn't get a girlfriend, who knows what he'll do?"

"So Roy's going to walk me until he finds a girl-friend?" I asked. "I'll never get to stop and sniff another tree for as long as I live!"

Dee Dee rubbed her chin and thought for a moment. Then she said, "Roast beef."

"What?"

"I'm going to the store tomorrow to get a pound of sliced roast beef," she said. "Every time Roy takes you for a walk, you'll get a slice."

My eyes widened. Just the thought of roast beef made my mouth start to water. "You promise?"

"I promise," Dee Dee said.

"When do we start?" I asked eagerly.

Five

The next morning at breakfast, Dee Dee limped into the kitchen on crutches with a large bandage on her ankle. Flora and Leyland looked very surprised.

"Dee Dee, darling, what happened?" her mother asked.

"I twisted my ankle," Dee Dee said.

"But it was fine last night when you went to bed," Leyland said.

"I, er, must have done it in my sleep," Dee Dee said.

The rest of the family gave each other puzzled looks.

"How could you twist your ankle in your sleep?" Roy asked.

"Uh, sleepwalking?" Dee Dee said.

"But then who put the bandage on?" Flora asked.

"I don't know," Dee Dee said. "I woke up and there it was."

"Maybe the ankle fairy did it," Janine said with a smirk.

"I don't understand," said Leyland.

"Well, if I could walk in my sleep, I guess I could put a bandage on in my sleep, too," Dee Dee said.

Janine shook her head and sighed. "This family is *so weird*."

Meanwhile, Dee Dee turned to Roy. "I need to ask you a super-big favor. Could you please walk Wordsworth after breakfast?"

Roy made a face. "Why can't you?"

"On crutches?" Dee Dee asked. "What if he smells something good to eat and starts to pull really hard on the leash? I'll go straight down on my face."

"Then just let him out in the backyard," Roy said. He obviously didn't want to walk me.

"Please walk him, Roy," Dee Dee begged. "I'll be your best friend."

"I don't want you for my best friend," Roy said.

"We're a family, Roy," Leyland reminded him. "We help each other in times of need."

"Then why can't someone else in the family walk him?" Roy asked.

"Because we're a family where Roy walks the dog when Dee Dee can't," Janine said with a smile.

Six

Being walked by Roy was not fun. Even though Dee Dee talked to him about letting me stop to sniff things, Roy wouldn't let me stop for long.

"Come on, you dumb dog," he grumbled every time I stopped to sniff anything. Then he'd pull my leash before I had time to get in one good whiff. I wanted to explain to him that sniffing is an art. You don't just take one sniff and leave. You sniff on the approach. You sniff at the location. And you sniff as you depart. There's a lot of information to gather and you can't get it all in one noseful.

"Come on, you dumb dog." Once again he yanked at my leash.

But try telling Roy that.

We went into the park. It was filled with people. There were lots of unfamiliar kids around, waiting for their chance to race that afternoon. I stopped to smell a large rock.

Wordsworth and the Roast Beef Romance

"I can't believe Dee Dee," Roy complained. Like most people, he sometimes talks to me, but he doesn't expect an answer. "I bet there's nothing wrong with her ankle. She has to be faking. She's—"

Roy stopped in midsentence. I looked up from the rock. A group of girls was coming down the path toward us. *Perfect*, I thought. *Maybe one of them will become Roy's girlfriend. Then he'll never have to walk me again.*

"Come on, Wordsworth." Roy tugged on my leash. "Let's go this way."

He started pulling me *away* from the girls. He'd never find a girlfriend that way.

So I pulled back. *Toward* the girls.

"Wordsworth!" Roy gasped. "Not that way. *This* way!"

Sorry, Charlie. I was a dog with a mission. I dug my nails into the ground and eighty-five pounds of basset hound started toward the girls.

Roy had no choice but to follow.

The group of girls saw me coming. I guess they also saw Roy being dragged behind me. No one said what a cute dog I was. No one asked if she could pet me. I kept going until I was right in the middle of them. Then I stopped and sat down.

The girls looked at me, then at Roy, who was still holding the leash. No one said a word.

"Uh, sorry," Roy stammered. "I don't know what got into him."

The girls nodded.

"He usually doesn't act this way," Roy said. He gave the leash a sharp tug. "Come on, Wordsworth, let's go."

I just sat there and didn't budge.

"Wordsworth! Now!" Roy pulled harder. But he didn't have a prayer.

"Guess he doesn't want to go," one the girls said.

"Well, good luck," said another girl.

The girls started to walk down the path. I got up and walked just ahead of them. Once again, Roy had no choice except to follow. Only now he was in the middle of all the girls.

The girls started to give each other funny looks.

"I really don't understand it," Roy said.

"Does he always do this?" one girl asked.

"No, never," Roy said. "I mean, I don't really know. I hardly ever walk him."

"He's your dog, isn't he?" asked another girl.

"Well, he's really my sister's," Roy explained. "But she twisted her ankle. I mean, she *says* she twisted her ankle. I don't really believe her."

"Why not?" one of the girls asked.

"Because she says she twisted it in her sleep," Roy said. "And somehow it got bandaged in her sleep, too."

The girls gave each other more strange looks.

"That's an interesting story," said one of them.

"Well, you never know," Roy said. "In my family, anything is possible."

"That's no surprise," one of the girls said. Then she winked at the other girls and they smiled.

The girls kept walking. I kept walking. Roy kept walking. No one said a word. Roy was never going to find a girlfriend this way.

"Can't you make him do *anything?*" one of the girls finally asked. A few of the other girls snickered. I realized there was no point in walking with them anymore. They were only going to get mean. So I turned toward a park bench and stopped.

Roy stopped and waved at the girls. "Well, bye."

The girls continued down the path without saying a word.

Roy sat down on the bench. He hunched his shoulders and hung his head.

"I can't believe you did that, Wordsworth," he groaned. "Do you have any idea how *embarrassing* that was?"

I looked up and gave him my saddest basset-hound look. I really hadn't meant to embarrass him. But hey, I was only doing my job.

"I mean, those girls were laughing at me," Roy said. "I wanted to die."

I felt bad for him. But how else was I going to get my roast beef?

"Well, that's it," Roy said. "That's *the last time* I ever walk you."

Uh-oh. It looked like my plan had backfired. If Roy wouldn't walk me, I wouldn't get any roast beef!

And then it happened. A voice said, "Wow, what an amazing dog!"

It was a girl's voice.

Seven

Roy and I both looked up. A girl was standing on the path, looking at me. She had short blond hair and large brown eyes and a cute turned-up nose. She was smiling.

"Can I pet him?" she asked.

"Sure." Roy shrugged.

She came toward me and kneeled down. I quickly rolled over on my back.

"He wants his tummy scratched," the girl said.

"Yeah," said Roy. He sounded thoroughly depressed.

The girl scratched my tummy.

"How old is he?" she asked.

"Uh, I think about three," Roy said.

"Is this his full size?"

"It'd better be."

"He seems really nice," she said. "Is he?"

"Well, he's okay," Roy said.

She kept asking questions about me. Gradually Roy must have realized that she wasn't going to make fun of him like the other girls had. He started to grow more interested in her. Soon he was the one asking the questions.

"Are you here for Race Week?" he asked.

"Yup." She was scratching me behind my ears now. "I'm racing in the laser class. How about you?"

"I just sail for fun," Roy said.

"Then you must live around here," the girl said.

"Yeah, about a block away."

"It's beautiful here," she said.

"Where do you come from?" Roy asked.

"The other side of Bell Island Sound," the girl said. "But I'm staying here this week with a family. By the way, my name's Ruth Hazel Sherman. Everyone calls me Razel."

"Razel?" Roy frowned.

"It's short for Ruth Hazel," she said.

"Oh, I get it." Roy smiled. It was the first time I'd seen him smile in months. "My name's Roy. Roy Chandler."

"I've never met anyone named Roy before," Razel said. "How'd you get that name?"

"My father was a big fan of Roy Rogers."

"Who?"

"He was this cowboy on TV about a million years ago," Roy said. "I think he used to sing."

Razel was scratching me under my chin. I could tell

she was a nice human by the way she scratched me. I hoped she kept talking to Roy. I'd never been scratched that well by anyone but Doo Doo.

"I was named after my grandmothers," Razel said. "One was named Ruth and the other was named Hazel."

"I think I've met someone named Ruth before," Roy said. "But I'm pretty sure I've never met anyone named Hazel. And I've definitely never met a Razel before."

"Not many people have," Razel said.

She and Roy smiled at each other. Then Razel stopped scratching me and stood up.

"Well, guess I'd better get going," she said. "I've got a race this afternoon. Nice meeting you."

Roy looked as disappointed as I felt.

"Nice meeting you too," he said.

Razel started away. Then stopped. "Oh, Roy?"

"Uh, yeah?" Roy quickly looked up.

"What's his name?" She pointed at me.

"Wordsworth," Roy said. "He was named after some poet."

Not just *some* poet, I wanted to shout. One of the greatest poets who ever lived! The man who wrote:

> *I wandered lonely as a cloud*
> *That floats on high o'er vales and hills,*
> *When all at once I saw a crowd,*
> *A host, of golden chicken wings.*

Or something like that.

Anyway, Razel waved and said, "See you around." Then she walked away.

Roy sat on the bench and watched her go. He seemed like he was in a daze. After a few moments Razel disappeared down the path. Then Roy heaved a big sigh.

"Razel," he said in a wistful tone. He had a dreamy, distant look in his eyes.

He'd just fallen in love.

Eight

As soon as we got home I climbed the stairs to Dee Dee's room. She was sitting on her bed, drawing a picture of a lion. Her foot was still wrapped in the bandage.

"It worked!" I whispered.

"Huh?" She looked puzzled. "What worked?"

"Roy fell in love."

"What? Already!" Dee Dee's jaw dropped in surprise. "Oh, my gosh!"

She jumped off the bed, hurried to the door, and closed it. "Tell me what happened," she whispered.

I told her about how we'd met Razel.

"I can't believe it!" Dee Dee gasped. "What's her last name?"

"Sherman," I said.

"What family is she staying with?"

"Uh, I don't know."

"So what's going to happen next?" Dee Dee asked.

"I get my roast beef, remember?"

"No, I mean with Roy and Razel," she said.

"I don't know," I said. At that point I was more interested in getting my slice of roast beef.

"Are they going to see each other again?"

"Uh . . ." How was I supposed to know?

"Wordsworth, it's great that Roy's in love," Dee Dee said. "But if Razel doesn't become his girlfriend, he's just going to be unhappier."

I understood that there might be complications. But I was hungry.

"Can't I have my roast beef?" I asked.

"Of course you can," Dee Dee said. "You did your job."

We went downstairs and into the kitchen. Roy was there. He was sitting at the kitchen table, doodling on the back of an envelope and gazing out the window.

"Hi, Roy," Dee Dee said.

"Oh, uh, hi." Roy quickly hid the envelope.

"What were you writing?" Dee Dee asked as she pulled open the refrigerator.

"Nothing," Roy said, sliding the envelope into his pocket.

"So, did you and Wordsworth have a nice walk today?" Dee Dee asked as she took out the roast beef and put a slice in my food bowl. It smelled fabulous! I ate it quickly. It was nice and rare, just the way I like it!

"It was okay," Roy said.

"Anything interesting happen?" Dee Dee asked.

"Huh? Oh, uh, not really."

Dee Dee looked at me and winked because she knew her brother wasn't telling the truth.

"Hey," Roy said, "where are your crutches?"

Dee Dee looked surprised. She'd been so excited about Roy falling in love that she'd forgotten them!

"My ankle's much better," she said.

"Does that mean you want to start walking Wordsworth again?" Roy asked.

Groof! I quickly barked and shook my head. Roy might have been a terrible dog walker, but if he stopped walking me, I wouldn't get any more of that wonderful roast beef.

"You can still walk him if you like," Dee Dee said.

"Great!" Roy looked excited. Then he caught himself and calmed down. "Er, I mean, it's not as bad as I thought it would be."

"I'm so glad." Dee Dee smiled.

Brinnnggg! The phone started to ring.

"I'll get it!" Roy lunged for the phone. "Hello?"

His face fell. "No, she's not here. Yeah, I'll tell her. Bye." He hung up.

"Some guy looking for Janine?" Dee Dee guessed.

"Yeah." Roy nodded.

"Did you think it would be someone else?" Dee Dee asked.

"Uh, no, not really." Roy turned to leave the kitchen. "I gotta go upstairs."

As he left, the envelope he'd been doodling on fell

out of his pocket and onto the floor. As soon as he was gone Dee Dee scooped it up.

"Look, Wordsworth," she whispered. Only one word was written on the envelope. But it had been written over and over again until the letters became fat and dark.

The word was Razel.

"You're right!" Dee Dee whispered. "Roy *is* in love!"

Nine

Later that afternoon I was awakened from a nap to find Roy holding my leash.

"Come on, Wordsworth, time for another walk," he said.

Two walks in one day? He had to be kidding. I rolled over and closed my eyes.

"Hey, I mean it." Roy kneeled down and clipped the leash to my collar. Then he gave it a tug. "Come on."

I opened my eyes and gave him a sad look.

"We're going for a walk if it kills me," Roy said stubbornly.

It wouldn't kill him, but it might kill me. On the other hand, I knew there'd be a nice slice of roast beef waiting when we returned. I yawned and slowly got to my feet. Then I stretched and scratched myself. Roy watched impatiently.

"Are you *ready* yet?" he asked.

Hey, what was the rush? He should have been honored that I agreed to take another walk with him. Frankly, if there hadn't been another slice of roast beef at the other end, I would have gone back to sleep.

We went outside and headed for the park. Roy walked so fast I practically had to jog to keep up with him. Once again, Bell Island Sound was filled with sailboats. Sailboat watchers were sitting on the rocks. Roy went up to an older man and woman and asked if the lasers had finished racing.

"Ended about an hour ago," the man said.

"Thanks," Roy said. We started to walk away. "You hear that, Wordsworth? Razel's race ended an hour ago. Maybe she'll take another walk in the park."

We walked around the park for a while. Then we sat down on the bench where Roy had sat that morning. People stopped to pet me. Some girls even stopped to ask Roy about me. Roy answered them politely and then gazed back up the path, hoping Razel would come.

Time passed.

More people stopped to pet me and ask questions.

But none of them was Razel.

"She has to come, Wordsworth," Roy said with a slight hint of desperation in his voice. "What am I gonna do if she doesn't?"

Take me home so I can have another piece of roast beef, I thought.

Finally dinnertime came. Razel didn't come. The park started to empty out. Roy heaved a heavy sigh.

"Guess it's time to go home," he said. He sounded really sad. I have to admit that I was delighted. Now I could look forward to that roast beef *and* my regular lamb chop.

I practically had to drag Roy home. He kept looking back toward the park, as if hoping Razel might still show up.

The Chandlers were all in the kitchen when we got home. Without a word, Roy got out the bread and peanut butter and jelly. He went to the kitchen counter and started to make himself a large sandwich. Dee Dee gave me a look as she put my lamb chop in my food bowl.

"Was Razel there?" she whispered.

I shook my head.

The family sat down to eat. The phone rang. Roy jumped up to get it.

"If it's a boy, I'm not here," Janine said.

"Hello?" Roy said eagerly. Then his face fell. He glanced at Janine out of the corner of his eye. "Uh, sorry, she's not here . . . Yeah, I'll tell her you called. Bye."

Roy slumped back into his chair. Janine bit into the sub she'd bought at the sub shop.

"Don't you want to know who it was?" Leyland asked.

"No," Janine said.

Meanwhile, Flora turned to Roy. "Usually you don't answer the phone."

Roy just shrugged. The phone rang again. Everyone looked at each other.

"Aren't you going to answer it?" Dee Dee asked Janine.

"Let the phone machine get it," Janine said.

We listened as the phone machine answered and some young man with a quivering voice left a message for Janine.

"They never give up," Janine said with a sigh.

"You should appreciate the fact that so many guys like you," Roy said.

"I used to appreciate it," Janine said. "Now it's just a pain."

"I have an idea," Flora said. "Why don't we make our phone number unlisted? Then the boys won't bother Janine so much."

"No!" Roy gasped. "What if someone wants to call me or Dee Dee?"

"We'll still give out our phone number to our friends," Flora said.

"But maybe someone who isn't our friend will want to call," Roy said.

"Why would someone who isn't our friend call?" Leyland asked.

"Well, maybe they're not our friend *yet*," Roy said. "But that doesn't mean they won't become our friend someday."

Everyone looked puzzled. Dee Dee winked at me again. We both knew Roy was thinking about Razel.

"Then perhaps we should give Janine her own phone and number," Leyland said. "It will ring only in her room, and the rest of us won't be bothered."

"That sounds okay," Janine said. The others agreed that it was a good idea.

"And I have some other news," Leyland said. "I have almost finished my latest invention."

"What's it this time?" Janine asked.

"It's a wind-seeking device," Leyland explained. "It fits any size sailboat. It automatically steers the sailboat to the strongest wind. I call it the Auto Wind Find."

"But then there's nothing for the sailor to do," Janine said.

"Only when it's turned on," Leyland said. "Think of it as an autopilot, like a plane has. You turn it on only when you don't feel like steering for a while."

"I think it sounds like a wonderful idea," said Flora. "Roy, what do you think?"

"Huh?" Roy looked up.

"What do you think of your father's latest invention?" his mother asked.

"What invention?" Roy asked.

"He just described it," Flora said. "Weren't you listening?"

"I must've missed it." Roy shrugged.

Dee Dee gave me a knowing look. Roy must have been dreaming about Razel.

Flora's forehead wrinkled. "Roy, dear, are you feeling all right?"

"Uh, okay, I guess."

"If I didn't know better, I'd say he was in love," Janine said with a smile.

"I am not," Roy insisted.

"Now, dear," Flora said to Janine. "Don't tease your brother."

Dee Dee finished her dinner. "I'm going upstairs," she said. "Come on, Wordsworth."

I didn't move. She'd forgotten something.

Dee Dee frowned at me. "I said come on."

I got up, but instead of following her, I walked over to the refrigerator and scratched at the door with my paw.

"I just gave you dinner," Dee Dee said.

"Wordsworth is getting greedy," Janine said.

It wasn't true. I just wanted what I deserved. Suddenly Dee Dee understood.

"Later, Wordsworth, I promise," she said.

I gave her a look. Dee Dee rolled her eyes. "I *swear*."

"What is with those two?" Janine asked.

"Now, now," Flora said. "Dee Dee and Wordsworth have a special relationship."

"I'll say," Janine said.

I followed Dee Dee out of the kitchen. We went into the den and she shut the door.

"I know I owe you a slice of roast beef for the second walk," she whispered. "I promise I'll give it to you as soon as they leave the kitchen. Now tell me what happened this afternoon."

Wordsworth and the Roast Beef Romance

I told her Roy had waited for Razel, but she never came.

"What if she doesn't take another walk in the park this week?" Dee Dee whispered. "Then she'll go home without ever speaking to Roy again. He'll be heartbroken."

"Can't he see her anyplace but the park?" I asked.

"That's it!" Dee Dee gasped, and hugged me around the neck. "We'll arrange a date!"

Ten

"A date?" I said.

"Yes. Come on." Dee Dee headed for the den door.

"Wait a minute," I said. "Where are we going?"

"To the yacht club."

"What about my roast beef?" I asked.

"I promise I'll give it to you when we come back," she said.

"That's not fair."

"Everyone's still in the kitchen," Dee Dee said. "I can't give it to you until they leave."

"I'll wait," I said.

"But the desk at the yacht club closes at six," Dee Dee said.

"So you go."

"You know Mom and Dad don't like me to go outside in the evening alone," Dee Dee said.

"But I've already had two walks today," I said. "That exceeds my daily quota."

Wordsworth and the Roast Beef Romance

Dee Dee put her hands on her hips and gave me an impatient look. "For Pete's sake, Wordsworth. This is important."

"To whom?" I asked.

"Oh, all right." Dee Dee said. "Come with me to the yacht club and you'll get *two* slices of roast beef when we get back."

"Now you're talking," I said.

Dee Dee got my leash and told her parents she was taking me for a walk. Then we headed for the front door.

"Hey, wait up!" Roy called behind us.

Dee Dee and I turned around. Roy jogged down the hall from the kitchen.

"Where're you going?" he asked Dee Dee.

"I thought we'd walk over toward the yacht club," Dee Dee said.

"No kidding." Roy opened the front door and held it for Dee Dee and me. Then he closed it and followed us out onto the porch.

"Listen," he said in a low voice. "There's something I want to talk to you about. But you have to swear you won't tell anyone."

"Okay," Dee Dee said.

"And you have to swear you won't make fun," Roy added.

"I swear," said Dee Dee.

Roy took a deep breath and let it out slowly. "Well, there's this person."

"Person?" Dee Dee frowned and pretended not to understand.

"Well, she's a girl, actually," Roy explained. "Her name's Razel. That's short for Ruth Hazel. She's a little taller than you and she has short blond hair and brown eyes. And she's really nice. And, well, if you happen to see her, could you say hello for me?"

"That's it?" Dee Dee said. "Just say hello? Can't I say you'd like to see her?"

"*No!*" Roy gasped.

"Why not?" Dee Dee asked.

"Because you can't," Roy said. "Just say hello. That's all."

"Oh, I get it," Dee Dee said. "You're afraid of rejection."

Roy's face turned red. "Look, all I'm asking is that you say hello if you see her, okay? That's it."

"Sure, if that's the way you want it. Come on, Wordsworth." Dee Dee led me down the porch steps and toward the yacht club. It was a few blocks away, but I'd already done a lot of walking that day and my legs were tired. The only thing that kept me going was the thought of those two slices of roast beef.

"Can you believe Roy asked me to say hello to her?" Dee Dee said as we walked. "He must really be in love."

"Is it contagious?" I asked.

"Not unless there's a cute female basset hound around," Dee Dee said.

Wordsworth and the Roast Beef Romance

It wasn't long before we arrived at the yacht club. We walked in the gate and down the long driveway, past the broad green lawn and the red clay tennis courts. The yacht club itself is housed in a large brown wood building with a red roof. It looks like a huge old mansion.

Most of the time the yacht club is pretty quiet inside. The brown wood walls are lined with miniature models of white sailboat hulls, and people sit on couches and talk quietly. But during Race Week it's always crowded and noisy. Dee Dee led me up to the front desk, where a young woman was sitting.

"Excuse me," Dee Dee said. "I have a friend who comes here every year to race. Her name's Ruth Hazel Sherman. Can you tell me who she's staying with this year?"

The woman behind the desk opened a large book and looked through it. "Here she is. Ruth Hazel is staying with the Kavanaughs."

"Great," Dee Dee said. "And by the way, what time does the clambake start tomorrow night?"

"Five-thirty."

"Okay, thanks." Dee Dee led me back out of the yacht club and we headed for home.

"Now we know where she's staying," Dee Dee said.

"Are you going to tell Roy?" I asked.

"No," said Dee Dee. "He's much too shy to call her."

"Then what are you going to do?"

"I'm not going to do anything," Dee Dee said. "*You are.*"

"Me?" I said. "What can I do?"

"You can call Razel," Dee Dee said.

Eleven

〰〰〰

"Call her?" I gasped. "Are you crazy?
I'm a dog."

"So? She won't know that."

"But I don't sound anything like Roy," I said.

"Don't worry, I can take care of that," Dee Dee
said.

"Well, I'm not doing *anything* until I get my two
slices of roast beef," I said.

"I know, Wordsworth," Dee Dee said. "Believe me,
I know."

As soon as we got back to the Chandlers' Roy came
down the stairs.

"You didn't happen to see her, did you?" he asked
hopefully.

"Sorry." Dee Dee shook her head.

Roy's shoulders sagged and he looked very disappointed. "Well, thanks anyway." He turned and headed
slowly back up the stairs.

45

"Wow, I've never seen him like this," Dee Dee whispered as we went into the kitchen.

The kitchen was empty. Dee Dee took out my two slices of roast beef and put them in my food bowl. Then she took out the Soundview Manor phone book.

"Kavanaugh . . . here they are!" She pointed into the phone book.

I didn't bother to look. I was too busy giving the roast beef my full attention.

"Okay, Wordsworth," Dee Dee said. "I'll call the Kavanaughs and hold the phone for you. You ask for Razel Sherman."

"And say, 'Hi, this is the eighty-five pound basset hound you met the other day'?" I said.

"Of course not," Dee Dee said. "You say you're Roy."

"But I don't sound like Roy."

"Then say you've got a sore throat."

"And then what?" I asked.

"Ask if she's going to the clambake tomorrow night," Dee Dee said. "If she says yes, tell her you'll see her there."

"And if she says no?" I asked.

"I don't know," said Dee Dee. "Make something up."

"I think this is going to cost you another piece of roast beef," I said.

"Don't be a pig, Wordsworth," Dee Dee said.

"I'm not a pig," I said. "I'm a basset hound. A hungry basset hound."

Wordsworth and the Roast Beef Romance

"You had dinner half an hour ago," Dee Dee said. "And you just had two slices of roast beef."

"This has been a hard day for me," I said. "I need sustenance."

"You need to go on a diet," Dee Dee said.

"No roast beef, no phone call," I said.

"Okay, you win." Dee Dee rolled her eyes. Then she reached for the phone and dialed the Kavanaughs' number. "Here." She held the phone next to my ear. "Can you hear it ring?"

"It would help if you held it *under* my ear," I said.

"Oh, right." Dee Dee lifted my ear and held the phone under it. I could hear it ringing.

"Ahem." I heard someone clear their throat. But they weren't on the phone. They were in the kitchen. Dee Dee and I both looked up. It was Janine!

"Would someone like to tell me what's going on?" she asked.

Twelve

———

Dee Dee quickly took the phone from
my ear and hung it up.

"Well?" Janine said.

"Uh, we were just playing," Dee Dee said inno-
cently.

"Playing telephone?" Janine raised an eyebrow.

"Yup."

"Let me guess," said Janine. "You're teaching
Wordsworth to call out for pizza."

"How'd you know?" Dee Dee asked.

Janine just shook her head. "What did I do to
deserve such a strange family?" She walked out of the
kitchen.

Dee Dee glanced at me with wide eyes. "That was
close," she whispered. Then she dialed the phone again
and held it to my ear. The phone rang. Then a girl
answered.

"Hello?"

48

"Uh, hello, I'm calling for Razel Sherman," I said.

"Who shall I say is calling?" she asked.

"Maxwell Short Wordsworth the Sixth," I said.

"No!" Dee Dee hissed. "You're supposed to be Roy."

"Okay, I'll go get her," the girl on the phone said.

I gave Dee Dee an apologetic look. "Sorry," I whispered. "I forgot."

"Hello?" It was Razel.

"Oh, hi," I said.

"Who is this?" she asked.

"Uh, it's Roy Chandler," I said. Dee Dee smiled and nodded.

"Who?" Razel said.

"Roy," I said. "The boy you met in the park yesterday. With that handsome basset hound."

"Your name isn't Wordsworth?" Razel asked.

"No, it's Roy," I said. "My magnificent basset hound is named Wordsworth."

"You're so lucky to have a dog like that," Razel said.

"I know," I said. "Wordsworth is an exceptional and fantastic dog. And he loves people who feed him."

Dee Dee rolled her eyes and made a face.

"You know," Razel said, "you don't sound like Roy."

"Oh, uh, I've got a sore throat," I said.

"Sorry to hear that," Razel said.

"Ask about the race," Dee Dee whispered.

"Uh, how was the race?" I asked.

"It was okay," Razel said. "I came in fourth. I have to do a lot better tomorrow."

"Ask about the clambake," Dee Dee whispered.

"How was the clambake?" I asked.

"No!" Dee Dee hissed.

"Isn't the clambake tomorrow night?" Razel said.

"Ask if she's going," Dee Dee whispered.

"Are you going?" I asked.

"To the clambake?" Razel said. "Oh, sure."

"Tell her you'll see her there," Dee Dee whispered.

"I'll see you there," I said.

"Oh, okay. Think you'll bring Wordsworth?"

"Do they just serve clams?" I asked. I'm not a big seafood fan.

"Oh, no," Razel said. "There's chicken and hamburgers and hot dogs too."

"In that case I think Wordsworth will definitely be there," I said.

"Oh, good," Razel said. "See you then. Bye."

"Bye," I said.

Dee Dee took the phone away from my ear and hung it up.

"So she's going to the clambake?" she asked.

"Yup," I said. "And she's looking forward to seeing me there."

"Wordsworth, we're doing this for Roy, remember?" Dee Dee said.

"Mind if I ask a question?" I said.

"Go ahead."

"Why are you going through all this trouble for him?" I asked.

Dee Dee looked surprised. "Because he's my brother."

"Who usually ignores you when he isn't picking on you," I reminded her.

"I know." Dee Dee nodded and sighed. "But he's *still* my brother and I love him, and I believe that deep down he loves me. We have to take care of each other. Now let's go upstairs and tell him about the clambake."

"Ahem." I cleared my throat.

"What?" Dee Dee said.

"Aren't you forgetting something?"

"Oh, right." Dee Dee opened the refrigerator and took out another slice of roast beef. "You're a tough businessman, Wordsworth."

"Not tough," I said. "Hungry."

I ate that delicious slice of roast beef and followed Dee Dee upstairs. She knocked on her brother's door.

"Who is it?" Roy asked.

"Dee Dee. Can I come in, please?"

"Okay."

Dee Dee pushed open Roy's door. Comic books and cards were scattered around the floor. The television was on and Roy was standing in front of it, grunting as he lifted weights.

"What's up?" Roy asked.

"I have good news," Dee Dee said. "You know that girl, Razel?"

"Yeah?" Roy's eyes widened. He put down the weights.

"Well, I just found out that she's going to the clambake tomorrow night," Dee Dee said.

"Oh." Roy shrugged and started to pick up the weights again.

Dee Dee frowned. "Well, aren't you excited? That means you can see her."

"Forget it, Dee Dee," Roy said. "There's no way I'm going to see Razel at the clambake."

Thirteen

Dee Dee looked dumbfounded. "But I thought you wanted to see her."

"I do," Roy said. He lifted the weights over his head.

"Then why not see her at the clambake?"

"Because she'll be with all her friends," Roy said. "You know what happens when a girl's with her friends? She has to act cool, like she doesn't care."

"But not Razel," Dee Dee said. "You said she was nice."

"Doesn't matter." Roy grunted and jerked the weights up again. "Even nice girls change when they're with their friends."

"Why don't you just go to the clambake anyway?" Dee Dee asked. "If Razel's with her friends, you don't have to talk to her. If she's not with her friends, then you can talk to her."

"Forget it."

"Why not?" Dee Dee asked.

"Because I know what'll happen," he said. "Razel will be there with her friends. But when I see her I'll want to talk to her anyway. And then she'll act cool and I'll feel really dumb. It'll be horrible."

"Okay, then suppose I make sure you get to see Razel alone," Dee Dee said.

Roy looked at her. "How?"

"Don't worry," she said. "I have a plan. Just promise me you'll go."

"If you swear I can get to see Razel alone, I'll go," Roy said.

"Great," Dee Dee said. She started toward the door. "Come on, Wordsworth, let's go."

We left Roy's room and went into Dee Dee's. Dee Dee flopped down on her bed and stared at the ceiling. I pushed the door closed with my paw.

"What's your plan to get Roy and Razel alone?" I asked.

"I don't have a clue," Dee Dee said.

"But you swore," I said.

"That's right," Dee Dee replied. "And by tomorrow night, I'll think of something."

Fourteen

———— ∞∞∞ ————

The next evening, the whole Chandler
family walked over to the yacht club for the clambake.
The sun was just starting to set, and we could hear
music coming from the band the club always hires for
the occasion. Dee Dee led me on my leash.

"I don't recall that they allow pets at the clambake," Flora said.

"Wordsworth's not a pet," Dee Dee said. "He's a
member of the family."

"Only someone in *our* family would say that,"
Janine said with a groan.

As we got to the yacht club gates the smoky scent
of grilling hamburgers and chicken wafted toward me.
I could tell this was going to be a wonderful evening.
Dee Dee stopped.

"You guys can go ahead," she said. "I need to talk
to Roy for a second."

Flora, Leyland, and Janine went ahead.

56

Wordsworth and the Roast Beef Romance

"So what's the plan?" Roy asked his sister.

"Don't do anything until it gets dark," Dee Dee said. "Then go over to the dock where the gas pumps are. Wait there and Razel will come."

"How do you know?" Roy asked.

"I'll arrange it," Dee Dee said.

"Right," Roy said with a smirk. "What are you going to do? Tell her I'm waiting for her?"

"No," Dee Dee said. "I promise you I won't say a word."

Roy stared at her for a second, then shrugged. "Okay, Dee Dee, I'm trusting you."

"Go in," Dee Dee said. "I'll be in soon."

Roy went into the yacht club. Dee Dee turned and walked me down the sidewalk along a high hedge. She waited until no one was around, then she bent down and started to pet me.

"Listen," she said in a low voice. "Mom was right. Dogs aren't allowed at the clambake."

"Then what am I going to do?" I asked.

"You'll have to wait until it's dark and sneak in through the hedge," Dee Dee said. "Go find Razel and pretend you're lost. But as soon as she takes your leash, lead her over to the dock where the gas pumps are."

"What if I get caught?" I asked.

"I don't think they'll do anything bad to you," Dee Dee said.

"Sounds pretty dangerous," I said. "I think I should get two slices of roast beef for this."

"Wordsworth, all this extra meat isn't good for you."

"Who says?" I asked.

"Doctors."

"That's just a myth perpetuated by the media, the scientific community, and the medical profession."

Dee Dee looked at me like I was crazy. "What?"

"Okay, okay, *one* slice," I said. "Take it or leave it."

"That's a deal," Dee Dee said. "Now just wait here until it gets dark."

"You mean you're not going to wait with me?" I asked.

"No, Mom and Dad expect me inside," she said. "But I'll see you later."

Dee Dee went in through the gate and left me alone by the hedge like some kind of lost dog. I sat there and waited. That wonderful scent of grilled meats was growing stronger. My mouth was starting to water, but I knew I wasn't supposed to sneak in until it was dark.

Besides, Dee Dee had promised me a slice of roast beef.

But I wouldn't get it until I got home.

The fabulous scent of those burgers and hot dogs was driving me crazy. I might starve if I waited until we got home.

Those hamburgers smelled so good. . . .

Maybe I could sneak in a little early. Basset hounds are low to the ground. I might not be noticed.

Wordsworth and the Roast Beef Romance

I started to get up, but then stopped myself. Dee Dee had told me not to go in until it was dark. Otherwise I might get caught.

On the other hand, the roast chicken smelled wonderful.

I went through the hedge.

There were hundreds of people milling around the yacht club lawn. The women wore dresses and the men wore blue blazers and light-colored slacks. Many of them were standing on line for food. Cooks wearing white outfits stood behind long outdoor grills covered with sizzling meats. Behind the cooks were large cardboard boxes. Inside those boxes was more meat than most dogs see in a lifetime.

I sneaked behind a tree and considered my options. Usually I prefer cooked meats to raw. But it would have been almost impossible to get anything cooked off the grill without all those people seeing me. It looked like I'd be better off going for the uncooked food in the boxes.

That ruled out the chicken. I *hate* raw chicken.

Hamburger was a possibility. I enjoy steak tartare.

But the best choice was the hot dogs. Frankly, I find it hard to tell the difference between them cooked and uncooked.

I crept quietly up to the boxes behind the hot dog grill. The aroma was fabulous! I could practically taste those wonderful links in my mouth already.

I waited until the cooks had their backs to me.

Wordsworth and the Roast Beef Romance

Then I crawled up to the closest box. It was open! The scent of those hot dogs was thick and sweet. I rose up on my toes and prepared to plunge!

"Wordsworth!" someone gasped. "What are you doing here?"

Fifteen

※※※

It was Dee Dee, of course. Of all the rotten luck! She came around the boxes and quickly led me behind a large old oak tree, where we wouldn't be seen.

"You were trying to steal hot dogs!" she said angrily.

"No, I wasn't!" I said. "I was just trying to see how many come in a box."

Dee Dee gave me a look. "Why?"

"Well, in case I ever have my friends over for a cookout," I said.

"Give me a break," Dee Dee groaned. "And I thought I told you not to sneak in until it was dark. What if you got caught?"

"I'd just sneak in again," I said. "Anyway, it's almost dark. Have you seen Razel?"

"She's over there." Dee Dee pointed at a large crowd of girls and boys standing near the band. "But I really want you to wait until it gets dark."

I glanced back at the grill, wishing I could get my

paws on some of those hot dogs. Hmmm . . . That gave me an idea. "Okay, what should we do until then?"

"You're going to stay behind this tree where no one will see you," Dee Dee said.

"Alone?" I gave her a sad look.

"For Pete's sake, Wordsworth," Dee Dee said. "Since when do you need a babysitter?"

"Well, I don't, really," I admitted. "But I sure could use a hot dog."

"But you've already had all that roast beef, plus a lamb chop," Dee Dee said.

"This is dangerous work," I said. "I deserve hazard pay."

Dee Dee sighed. "You're just lucky I love you so much. Okay, wait here."

"Think you could make it two?" I asked as she turned away. "You never know. They may run out later."

The hot dog line wasn't very long. Dee Dee soon came back with two hot dogs.

"I didn't know whether you wanted mustard or catsup so I got one with each," she said.

"Perfect."

Dee Dee patted me on the head. "You're a good dog, Wordsworth. A *hungry* dog, but a good dog too."

By the time I'd finished both hot dogs, I really was full. Dee Dee had rejoined her parents. At my hiding spot behind the tree, the grass was soft and the air was fresh. I soon felt an undeniable urge to sleep. *Oh, well*, I thought, *a little nap won't hurt*.

• • •

"Wordsworth, wake up!" someone hissed.

I opened my eyes. Dee Dee was looking down at me in the dark.

"You're supposed to be leading Razel to Roy," she said.

"Later." I yawned and closed my eyes.

"No, now," Dee Dee insisted. "We made a deal."

"I had my fingers crossed," I mumbled.

"You don't have fingers," Dee Dee said. "Now get going."

I got up and wound my way through dozens of legs until I came to the group Razel was in. Nobody noticed me in the dark so I rubbed against her leg.

"Oh, wow, look who's here," she said, looking down.

Groof! I gave her a short bark and an eager smile.

"Aren't you with Roy or Dee Dee?" she asked.

Groof! I shook my head. I wanted her to think I was lost.

"Okay, Wordsworth." Razel bent down and picked up the end of my leash. "I'll help you find them."

As soon as Razel got hold of the leash I started to pull.

"Hey, wait a minute!" she cried. "I thought *I* was going to take *you*!"

Not unless you're going to the dock, I thought. That's where I went.

The dock was empty and lit by a light every twenty feet.

Wordsworth and the Roast Beef Romance

"Why are we going out on the dock?" Razel asked.

You'll see, I thought.

As we went out we could hear the sound of waves sloshing against the pilings. Soon I saw a lone figure at the end of the dock. Razel must have seen him, too, because she started to slow down.

"Who's that, Wordsworth?" she asked nervously.

I kept pulling, but Razel followed more slowly. Roy was standing at the end of the dock with his back to us. Then he must have heard us, because he turned.

"Roy!" Razel gasped, surprised.

"Razel!" Roy looked surprised, too. I guess he didn't think Dee Dee was going to make good on her promise.

"What are you doing here?" Razel asked.

"I, er, was just looking at the moon," Roy said. He pointed at the moon, which was just starting to rise in the dark sky over Bell Island Sound. "What are you doing here?"

"I found Wordsworth," Razel said. "He seemed lost, so I said I'd try to find you or Dee Dee. But then he dragged me out here."

"Amazing," Roy said.

"Well." Razel smiled in the moonlight. "You said you'd see me here and you were right."

"I was?" Roy looked puzzled.

"Remember?" Razel said. "On the phone last night?"

Uh-oh, I thought.

"No." Roy shook his head.

"Don't you remember we talked on the phone?" Razel said. "You asked if I was coming to the clam-bake."

"No, I didn't," Roy said.

Razel frowned. "You did, Roy. And what happened to your sore throat?"

"What sore throat?" Roy asked.

"Last night on the phone," Razel said. "You sounded different. You said you had a sore throat."

"I'm sorry, Razel," Roy said. "I didn't call you and I didn't have a sore throat."

"Then someone played a trick on me," Razel said.

Suddenly Roy blinked. "So *that's* how she knew!"

Sixteen

"Who?" Razel asked. "Knew what?"

"Uh, I can't explain now," Roy said. "I'm really sorry, Razel. I had nothing to do with this."

"With what?" Razel asked.

"I . . . I have to go," Roy said. He took my leash and we started down the dock.

"But it's not that important," Razel began.

I'm not sure Roy heard her. He was almost jogging. It wasn't easy to keep up with him, considering I had a full stomach. He led me down the dock and through the crowd at the clambake until we found Dee Dee. I had to sit down and catch my breath.

"Can I talk to you for a second?" Roy asked angrily.

"Where's Razel?" Dee Dee asked, looking around.

"On the dock."

"Then why aren't you with her?" Dee Dee asked.

"Because I'm here," Roy said. "It turns out someone called her last night and pretended to be me with a sore throat. I wonder who that could have been?"

"Uh . . ." Dee Dee glanced nervously at me.

"I can't believe you, Dee Dee," Roy said.

"I was only trying to help," Dee Dee said.

"Help?" Roy sputtered. "The only thing you helped me do was look like an idiot."

"But—" Dee Dee started to say.

"Listen, just stay out of my life, okay?" Roy snapped. "Mind your own business."

Then he turned and marched away into the dark.

Dee Dee looked down at me. "Follow him, Wordsworth."

"Forget it," I said, huffing and puffing. "I'm bushed. I've already had two walks, plus the trip to the yacht club *and* running up and down the dock. That's more exercise than I've had in years."

"I have to know where Roy goes."

"Since when am I the family spy?" I asked.

"Please?" Dee Dee begged.

"Well, I guess I could follow him," I said. "If I had something to keep me going."

Dee Dee stared at me. "You're impossible, Wordsworth."

"Could I have this one with sauerkraut?" I asked.

Dee Dee sighed. "Wait here."

She went off toward the hot dog grill. A moment later she returned with another hot dog.

"I'm just worried that you're going to get really fat," she said, giving me a hot dog heaped with sauerkraut.

Wordsworth and the Roast Beef Romance

"Tomorrow I'll go on a diet," I said, licking my lips.

"Now follow Roy?" Doo Doo asked.

"Your wish is my command," I said, and took off into the dark.

Seventeen

Seventeen

Being a relative of the bloodhound, I
quickly picked up Roy's scent. I assumed he would go
home. But I was wrong. He went down a different
street. I followed in the dark, wondering where he was
going. Finally we came to Soundview Manor Park. Roy
went down one of the paths through the trees. That was
strange. The only people who go into the park at night
are couples and bad kids like Adam Pickney, who
smoke cigarettes and spray graffiti on the rocks.

I followed Roy to a bench facing Bell Island
Sound. The moon hung in the sky above, and moonlight sparkled on the dark water. The sounds of music
and laughter drifted toward us from the yacht club.

On a bench not far away, a couple snuggled in the
darkness.

Roy sat on the bench with his elbows on his knees.
There wasn't much to spy on, so I decided to join him.
I trotted over and put my paws up on the bench.

Wordsworth and the Roast Beef Romance

"Hey, Wordsworth, what are you doing here?" Roy actually patted me on the head. He isn't usually that friendly, but maybe he was feeling lonely. I wondered if I could get a good tummy scratch out of this. But first I had to get up on the bench with him. I tried to jump up a couple of times, but I couldn't quite make it.

Yip! Yip! I had to get his attention.

"You want to get up here?" Roy asked. "Here you go."

He reached down and helped me onto the bench.

"Whew, Wordsworth, you are one heavy dog," he groaned.

Hey, it's all muscle, I thought. Then I lay down on my back with my head in Roy's lap. Roy got the idea and started to scratch my tummy. Man, this was the life. Lying in the moonlight with a belly full of hot dogs, getting a nice long tummy scratch. Sometimes it's great to be a dog.

"You know, Wordsworth, I really wish I had someone I could talk to," Roy said wistfully.

Well, I thought, *as long as you scratch, I'll listen.*

"I mean, about girls," he said. "The problem is, Mom and Dad are nice, but they might as well be from outer space. Janine would probably be good to talk to, but I'm always worried she'll make fun of me. And Dee Dee's too young to understand. She still thinks boys are gross."

He glanced over at the other bench, where the couple was snuggling.

Wordsworth and the Roast Beef Romance

"I just wish I knew what to do about Razel," Roy said. "I mean, I know I like her, but I never know what to say to her. Every time I see her, I just feel like a jerk."

I knew how he felt. There'd been a young Yorkshire terrier I'd liked once, but that was a long time ago.

"Razel seems really nice," Roy went on. "I don't think she'd laugh at me if I said something dumb. But I still don't know what to say. It's like my brain freezes every time I'm around her."

Roy was a good tummy scratcher. Maybe if he scratched Razel's tummy . . .

"You know what's really bad, Wordsworth?" he asked. "In a couple of days Race Week is going to be over and Razel's going to go home. I'll never see her again. I don't even know where she lives. I just wish there was some way I could let her know how I feel."

Maybe if he gave her some roast beef . . . Naw, humans don't seem to understand the joys of food the way we dogs do. Probably because they can have hot dogs and lamb chops and roast beef just about anytime they want.

On the bench near us, the couple snuggled closer and kissed. Roy let out a deep sigh, then got up. "Come on, Wordsworth, we'd better go home."

Eighteen

━━◈◈◈━━

Dee Dee and her parents were already
home when we got there. Janine was still at the clambake. Roy went up to his room to lift weights and
watch TV. I went into Dee Dee's room.

"What happened?" she whispered.

"He sat in the park," I whispered back.

"And?"

"He talked about how he wished he could talk to
Razel."

"Why can't he?" Dee Dee asked.

"He's too shy, I guess," I said.

"Did he say anything else?"

"Yes," I said. "He's unhappy because she's going to
go home in a few days."

"Hmmm." Dee Dee pressed her chin against her
arm. "It's not fair, Wordsworth. We have to help him."

I stretched and yawned. It had been a long day. I'd
done a lot of walking and I'd had a lot to eat. The rug

74

on Dee Dee's floor was soft and cozy. I lay down and closed my eyes.

"I know what we have to do," Dee Dee said.

"So do I," I said with another yawn. "We have to *sleep*."

"Get up, Wordsworth," she said. "We have to call Razel."

"Not now." I was on my way to dreamland.

"Oh, Wordsworth, don't go to sleep." Dee Dee reached over the side of the bed and shook my shoulder. "This is important."

"Sleep is important," I said.

"Wordsworth, if we don't do this, Roy's heart may get broken," Dee Dee said. "Do you want to see that happen?"

"It won't be the last time," I said. "It's a cruel world. He might as well get used to it."

"How can you be so heartless?" she asked.

"I'm not heartless, I'm sleepless," I muttered. *Sleepless in Soundview Manor* . . . Sounded like a movie. *Starring Maxwell Short Wordsworth the Sixth*. No, that sounded pretentious. How about Maxwell S. Wordsworth . . . or even M. Short Wordsworth? Hmmm, I'd have to work on that.

"I'm disappointed in you, Wordsworth," Dee Dee said. "You're being selfish. I thought you'd learned your lesson."

"I did," I said, and yawned again. "But being unselfish requires a certain amount of sleep. I'll see you in the morning."

"You can't go to sleep," Dee Dee said. "It may be too late by tomorrow morning. I'm serious, Wordsworth. We have to call her *now*!"

Dee Dee shook my shoulder again. It was obvious that I wasn't going to get any sleep until I made that call.

"Okay, okay," I grumbled, and stretched. "I'll do it. But it'll cost you a slice of roast beef."

"That's ridiculous," Dee Dee said. "You've already had three hot dogs and two slices of roast beef tonight. *Plus* your regular lamb chop. If you don't stop eating, you'll get so fat you won't be able to walk!"

"I'll become the world's first sumo-wrestling basset hound," I said. "The biggest, strongest basset hound in the world. You can call me Wordsworth-san."

"Get real." Dee Dee rolled her eyes.

"Okay, *half* a slice of roast beef," I said.

"Deal," said Dee Dee.

We went down to the kitchen. Dee Dee gave me my roast beef and coached me on what to say. Then she dialed the Kavanaughs' house and held the phone to my mouth.

"Hello?"

"Hi, is Razel Sherman there?" I said.

"Who's calling?"

"Uh, Roy Chandler."

"Just a minute."

A second later, Razel got on. "Hello, Roy?"

"Hi."

"You sound like the person who called last night and said they had a sore throat," Razel said.

"Uh, that's funny," I said.

"What happened to you tonight?" she asked. "How come you didn't stay and talk?"

"It's a long story," I said. "But I apologize for leaving without saying good-bye."

"Oh, well, that's okay."

"Ask her how the clambake was," Dee Dee whispered.

"So, uh, how was the clambake?" I asked.

"It was okay," Razel said. "I didn't know that many people so I didn't stay that long."

"Ask her what she's doing tomorrow," Dee Dee whispered.

"So, what are you doing tomorrow?" I asked.

"I've got a race tomorrow," she said. "What are you doing?"

"Tell her you might go sailing," Dee Dee whispered. "Maybe you'll see her on the Sound."

I looked back at her, surprised. "I thought Roy doesn't like to sail," I whispered.

"Just tell her," Dee Dee said.

I repeated what Dee Dee had told me about Roy going sailing.

"Great," Razel said. "Then maybe I'll see you tomorrow."

We hung up. I turned to Dee Dee. "How are you going to get Roy to sail?"

"Leave it to me," Dee Dee said.

Nineteen

_____ 🙰 _____

The next morning Leyland went to the
city early to visit his patent attorney. Whenever Leyland invents something new, he tries to have it
patented so that no one else can steal his idea.

Later, when Dee Dee and I came into the kitchen,
Roy was sitting at the kitchen table with his head
propped in his hands. He was moping.

"Hi, Roy," Dee Dee said cheerfully.

"Hi." Roy hardly looked up at her.

"Guess what?" Dee Dee said as she poured some
cereal into a bowl. "Dad said he'd take Wordsworth
and me sailing today and show us his new invention."

"I don't think so," Roy said. "Dad went to the city."

"What?" Dee Dee pretended to be shocked. "But
he promised!"

"You know Dad," Roy said with a shrug. "He
probably forgot."

"But I was really looking forward to it." Dee Dee
gave him a sad look.

78

"So you'll go tomorrow," Roy said.

"But I really want to go *today*," Dee Dee said.

Roy scowled at her. "What's with you? You usually don't care if you go sailing or not."

"But that's just it," Dee Dee said. "This was the one time I was really, really looking forward to sailing."

Roy shook his head. "Dee Dee, you are so weird."

"Would you take us?" Dee Dee asked.

"No way."

"I'm serious," Dee Dee said. "Take us, *please?*"

"Why?"

"Because we really want to go," Dee Dee said. "You don't have anything else planned, do you?"

"Well, not really," Roy admitted.

"Then please?"

"Can't you wait until tomorrow?" Roy had a pained look on his face.

"Well, I guess I could." Dee Dee gave me a wink. "But I thought it would be kind of neat to watch the sailboat races from out on Bell Island Sound. We might even see Razel out there."

"That's true." Suddenly Roy seemed to be considering the idea.

"Then what do you say?" Dee Dee asked eagerly.

"Oh, okay."

A little while later we went down to the yacht club. Leyland had installed the Auto Wind Find in the old sailboat a few days before. We all put on life preservers, including the special one they'd had made for me. It's shaped like a hot-dog roll with straps.

"Pretty gusty day," Roy said as we got into the sailboat. He and Dee Dee unfurled the sails and started to pull them up the mast. Soon the sails were flapping loosely in the wind. Bolted to the floor of the boat was the Auto Wind Find. It was about the size of a lawn mower. All the ropes from the sails went through it.

"Look." Dee Dee pointed toward Bell Island Sound, where dozens of sailboats were moving quickly in the wind. "Everyone's racing. I bet Razel's out there. I hope we can go watch her race."

"Maybe." Roy said. "Ready?"

"Aye-aye, captain!"

We started to sail away from the dock. I went up to the bow of the sailboat. That's my favorite place. I like to sit in the sun and sniff all the scents in the wind. And on days like that, when there's lots of wind and waves, I get to lick the salty sea spray off my nose.

Best of all, I don't have to run or fetch, or even walk.

Roy held the tiller and steered us. Dee Dee sat near him. Normally she would have held the ropes to the sail. But the Auto Wind Find was doing that instead. Pushed by the strong wind, the small old sailboat cut through the waves.

"Wow, this is amazing!" Roy shouted. "Dad's invention really does know how to find the strongest wind."

"Look!" Dee Dee pointed toward a group of small sailboats clustered tightly together. "Isn't that the laser class?"

"Looks like it," Roy said.

"Let's go see if Razel's there," Dee Dee said.

"Uh, okay," Roy said. "Only we don't want to get too close. We're not allowed to get in the way of the race."

We started to sail toward them. One sailboat was ahead of all the others.

"Roy, look!" Dee Dee pointed ahead. "I think I see Razel! She's in the lead!"

We kept sailing toward her.

"It's her!" Dee Dee yelled. "She's winning!"

We were coming closer and closer to the race. Now I could see Razel, sailing the lead boat. Her hair was tucked under a white cap and she was wearing an orange and yellow life preserver. Dee Dee came up to the bow next to me.

"Isn't this exciting, Wordsworth?" she asked.

Groof.

"Uh, Dee Dee?" Roy called from behind us.

Dee Dee turned and looked back at him. "What?"

"You know this Auto Wind Find?" Roy said.

"Uh-huh?"

"Do you know how to turn it off?"

Dee Dee frowned. "Don't you?"

"No."

The racing sailboats were about fifty yards away.

Wordsworth and the Roast Beef Romance

We were headed straight toward them. Razel was still in the lead.

"Maybe we'd better turn," Dee Dee said.

"I've been trying to." Roy pushed against the tiller, but the sailboat stayed on its course. "It's this Auto Wind Find. It won't let me change direction!"

"Then put out the anchor!" Dee Dee said.

"What anchor?" Roy asked.

"There's no anchor?" Dee Dee's eyes widened.

"Don't ask me," said Roy. "I haven't seen one."

"I'll look." Dee Dee pulled open the hatch in the bow of the sailboat and looked inside. Meanwhile we were still cutting through the waves, getting closer and closer to the race. This was what I called excitement!

Dee Dee looked up. "There's no anchor!"

By now we were only twenty-five yards from Razel's boat. She and some of the other racers had turned their heads and were watching us with curious expressions. They probably expected us to turn away at any moment.

Little did they know!

"We can't sail into the race!" Dee Dee cried. "We'll ruin everything!"

"No kidding!" Roy shouted back.

"What do we do?" Dee Dee asked.

"Uh . . . I know!" Roy cried. "Take down the sail!"

We were only fifteen yards away from Razel now. I saw the surprise on her face as she realized it was Roy and Dee Dee and me.

"Hurry!" Dee Dee shouted. She and Roy started untying the ropes that held up the sail.

But now we were ten yards and closing fast. Razel stared at us with wide eyes, as if she couldn't believe what she was seeing. The kids in the other sailboats were starting to shout and wave at us.

"Hey! This is a race!" "Turn away!" "Back off!"

Five yards.

"The sail's stuck!" Dee Dee cried.

We were so close to Razel that her eyes met mine.

"What are you doing?" she asked.

"Look out!" shouted Roy.

Crunk!

Twenty

The next thing I knew, I was flying through the air. It was fun . . . kind of.

Splash!

The water was cold. Thanks to my hot-dog-bun life jacket, I floated to the surface and bobbed up and down in the waves. What I saw wasn't pretty. Our sailboat had crashed into Razel's. For a moment the two boats were joined at their bows, as if they were kissing.

"Wordsworth!" Dee Dee shouted. She had also fallen into the water.

Behind her, Roy stood up in our sailboat. Razel was still in her boat. They were talking, but I couldn't hear what they were saying.

The strange thing was, Roy was getting shorter.

Dee Dee splashed toward me and put her arms around my neck. "Wordsworth, are you all right?"

"I think so," I whispered.

We bobbed up and down in the waves together. In the sailboat, Roy was getting even shorter!

"Why is Roy getting shorter?" I whispered.

"Huh?" Dee Dee's jaw dropped. "Oh, no! Roy's not getting shorter. The boat's sinking!"

Dee Dee was right. Leyland's sailboat was sinking lower and lower into the water. Roy was still standing in it. Like a good captain, he'd decided to go down with his ship!

Good thing he was wearing a life jacket!

"Get on my boat, Roy!" Razel yelled at him.

Roy didn't budge. His face was deep red. I think he was going to be the first sea captain ever who blushed as he went down with his ship.

"I'm really sorry, Razel," he said. "I mean, you can't believe how sorry I am. This is, like, the dumbest thing I've ever done. If it weren't for me, you would have won your race."

Razel turned to Dee Dee and me. "Here, let me help you out of the water."

Dee Dee swam toward Razel's sailboat. She was pulling me by my life jacket. I dog-paddled along next to her. We got next to the sailboat.

"Let me get Wordsworth." Razel reached down and tried to pull me out of the water. "He weighs a ton!"

Hey! That wasn't fair! It was only because my fur was wet!

"Let me help." Dee Dee grabbed the sailboat's gunwale and started to pull herself in. Razel helped her. Then they both turned toward me.

"Grab a paw," Dee Dee said.

Wordsworth and the Roast Beef Romance

They each grabbed one of my paws.

"Pull!" Dee Dee grunted.

They pulled. They groaned. They grimaced. Slowly but surely I slid over the gunwale until I was in Razel's sailboat. Both girls sat down and caught their breaths.

"I never thought we'd get him in the boat," Razel said.

"He's definitely going on a diet," gasped Dee Dee.

It seemed they'd forgotten about Roy for the moment. I barked at him.

"Oh, my gosh!" Razel gasped. "Roy!"

Both girls turned and looked at him. Roy was still standing in Leyland's sailboat. His arms were crossed. He wouldn't look at us. The sailboat was slowly filling with water. It was up to Roy's knees.

"Roy?" Razel said.

Roy wouldn't answer her.

"Roy, please get into Razel's boat," Dee Dee said.

Roy didn't reply.

"Roy, you can't go down with the ship," Dee Dee said. "You're wearing a life jacket."

Roy ignored her.

"Roy, I don't know what happened, but I'm sure you didn't do it on purpose," Razel said.

Leyland's sailboat was almost completely under water now. Only the mast, the sail, and Roy stuck out of the water.

"Roy, we'll tell Razel about the Auto Wind Find," Dee Dee said. "She'll understand."

Roy didn't budge. He, the mast, and the sail were all sinking faster now.

"You can't just stay in the middle of the Sound," Razel said.

The mast and sail continued to sink, but Roy stopped. He was floating in his life jacket now. The top of the mast slid past him and disappeared. Roy bobbed in the waves a few feet from Razel's sailboat. His arms were still crossed. He still wouldn't look at us.

"Do you think we could pull him in?" Dee Dee asked.

"Does he weigh more than Wordsworth?" Razel asked.

"Maybe a little more," said Dee Dee.

"Then we'll never get him in the boat," Razel said.

"What'll we do?" Dee Dee asked.

"I know." Razel picked up a piece of rope. "Tie this to the loop on the back of his life jacket."

Dee Dee reached over the side and tied one end of the rope to Roy's life jacket. Razel tied the other end to a cleat on her sailboat. Then she took the tiller and started to turn her boat back toward the harbor.

"Coming about," she said.

The sailboat turned and the sail filled with wind. We started to sail back to the harbor, dragging Roy in our wake.

Twenty-one

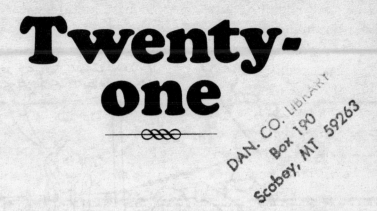

Roy was still floating in the water behind us when we arrived at the yacht club dock. His arms were still crossed. He still wouldn't look at us.

"Now what do we do?" Dee Dee asked.

"We can't just leave him in the water," Razel said.

"Maybe he'll feel better if I tell you what happened," Dee Dee said. Then she explained about the Auto Wind Find and how they couldn't turn it off.

"I'm really sorry about ruining your race," Dee Dee said. "It looked like you were winning."

Razel nodded. "I was. But it's okay. There's always tomorrow."

"Tomorrow's the last day of Race Week, isn't it?" Dee Dee asked.

"Yup." Razel nodded. "Tomorrow's the big race."

Dee Dee turned to Roy, who was still bobbing in the water. It looked like his lips were turning blue.

"Did you hear that, Roy?" she asked. "Razel still

has tomorrow's race. And she understands that the crash wasn't your fault."

Roy *still* wouldn't talk.

Razel leaned over the side of the sailboat. "Roy, you can't just float there forever. You'll freeze to death."

"Or a shark will get you," Dee Dee said.

"There are no sharks in Bell Island Sound," Roy replied.

Dee Dee turned to Razel. "Well, at least we know he can still talk."

"Roy, come on," Razel said. "This is silly. I know it wasn't your fault. I'm just sorry your sailboat sank."

Roy turned and looked at her. His teeth were chattering. "I just want you to know that it was Dee Dee's idea. She's the one who insisted we try the Auto Wind Find today."

"Gee, thanks for blaming *everything* on me," Dee Dee pouted.

"It's okay," Razel said. "Really. It doesn't matter."

They finally persuaded Roy to swim to the dock. Razel and Dee Dee helped him climb up. He stood on the dock, dripping water while he undid the life jacket.

"The least I can do is help you fix your boat," Roy said.

Razel walked along the dock to the front of her sailboat and looked. "To tell you the truth, it doesn't look like it was damaged."

"Oh, okay." Roy nodded. "Then I guess I'd better

go home and call Dad. He's not gonna be happy about this."

"I'll call him," Dee Dee said. "You can stay here."

"No, I'd better go home. I'm soaking wet," Roy said. He turned to Razel. "Well, good luck tomorrow."

"Thanks, Roy," Razel said.

Roy turned and walked down the dock, leaving a track of wet footprints behind. Dee Dee watched him sadly. I guess it looked like Roy and Razel were never going to get to know each other now.

Twenty-two

Dee Dee and I followed Roy home. He called the patent lawyer and found out that Leyland was already on his way back. Roy changed his clothes and sat on the front porch and waited for his father. Dee Dee and I watched him through the living room windows.

"He really looks depressed," Dee Dee said.

"He should be," I said. "He sank his father's sailboat, lost the Auto Wind Find, and ruined Razel's race."

"It's not his fault," Dee Dee said. "It's all my fault. If I hadn't interfered, none of this would have happened."

"True," I said.

Dee Dee glared down at me. "You're not supposed to say that, Wordsworth. You're supposed to tell me it's not my fault, either."

"Oops, sorry," I said. "I'll do that next time."

Dee Dee looked out the window at her brother again. "Maybe you should go outside and sit with him," she said. "Maybe you can find out what he's thinking."

"I don't have to go outside to know what he's thinking," I said. "He's thinking that he's in a ton of trouble."

"But I have to know what he's thinking about Razel," Dee Dee said.

"Maybe things would be better if we stayed out of it from now on," I said.

"We will stay out of it," Dee Dee said. "I'm just asking you to spy for me. There's a big difference."

"Yeah, right," I muttered, and went outside.

Roy didn't say a word when I came out. I lay down on the porch next to him. A few cars went by on Soundview Avenue. The gardeners were cutting Mayor Pickney's lawn next door.

"I've really blown it this time," Roy said sadly. "Razel will never forgive me. She'll probably never talk to me again. And Dad's gonna kill me when he finds out I sank his sailboat."

Frankly, I was still sort of amazed that the thing had floated in the first place.

"Know what?" Roy said with a sigh. "I don't think there's anything in the world that's worse than being a fourteen-year-old guy."

At least he wasn't a cat.

The Chandlers' old car pulled into the driveway

and Leyland got out. He was wearing a brown suit and a red tie. He climbed the steps that led to the front porch.

"Hi, Roy," he said.

"Hi, Dad," Roy said. "How was your day?"

"Terrific," Leyland said. "My lawyer thinks we'll have no problem winning a patent for the Auto Wind Find."

Roy winced.

"Why do you look so glum?" Leyland asked.

"I've got some really, really, totally bad news, Dad," Roy said.

Leyland looked worried. "Is everyone all right?"

"Oh, yeah," Roy said.

"Well, if everyone's all right and the house hasn't burned down, it can't be *that* bad," Leyland said.

"Dee Dee and I tried out the Auto Wind Find today," Roy said.

Leyland's forehead wrinkled. "It didn't work?"

"Oh, it worked great, Dad," Roy said.

"Then what was the problem?" Leyland asked.

"Well, you know how it's supposed to find the strongest wind?" Roy said.

"Yes."

"That's exactly what it did."

"But that's wonderful news," Leyland said.

"No, Dad," Roy said. "You see, once I'd turned the Auto Wind Find on, I couldn't turn it off."

"What happened?" Leyland asked.

"Well, you know the sailboat you bought?" Roy said.

"Yes."

"It sort of sank."

Leyland's eyebrows went up. "*Sort of?*"

"Well, you're right," Roy said. "It didn't sort of sink. It definitely sank."

"How?"

"Uh, it found the best wind in the same place that another sailboat did," Roy said. "So, they . . . like . . . crashed."

"Do you know where?" Leyland asked.

"Yeah, about a hundred yards due south of the point."

Leyland thought for a moment. "Well, then, that's not so bad."

Roy looked up at him. "Dad, didn't you hear me? I said the boat *sank*. With the Auto Wind Find on it."

"But we know where it sank, so we'll just go get it," Leyland said. "In the meantime, it sounds like the Auto Wind Find worked quite well."

Roy looked at him in wonder. "You mean you're not mad?"

"Of course not, Roy," Leyland said. "No permanent damage was done. That sailboat was practically a piece of junk. Meanwhile, we know my invention works. That's very good news. I'll go inside to call the harbor master. We'll get a salvage crew to find the boat and get the Auto Wind Find back."

Leyland went inside. Roy looked down at me again.

"Wow, Wordsworth," he said. "*That's a relief. At least Dad isn't mad.*" But then his shoulders slumped and he propped his chin in his hand. "Too bad Razel still hates me."

I got up and went back inside. Dee Dee was sitting on the couch, waiting.

"What happened?" she whispered.

"Your father isn't that upset about the sailboat," I whispered back.

"Did Roy say anything about Razel?"

"He's sure she hates him."

Dee Dee shook her head slowly. "It looks like we weren't much help. I think I've learned my lesson, Wordsworth. You were right. No more interfering with my brother's love life."

"Does that mean I won't be getting any more roast beef?" I asked. After all, I'd done my job.

"I'll let you finish what's left," Dee Dee said, rubbing my head.

Lucky me!

Twenty-three

The next morning was cloudy and windy. At breakfast the Chandlers stared out the kitchen window.

"Looks like we might be getting a storm," said Leyland. "I don't suppose they'll be able to salvage the sailboat in this weather."

"I think I'll paint inside today," said Flora.

"Looks like I won't be playing tennis," said Janine. "Maybe I'll go to the movies with Muffy."

"Guess I'll do the same thing I always do," Roy moped. "Watch TV and lift weights."

Dee Dee gave me a look. For a moment I wondered if she would change her mind and try to help her brother again.

"And what will you do, dear?" Flora asked her.

"Oh, I don't know," Dee Dee said. "I guess I'll take Wordsworth for a walk now in case it's stormy for the rest of the day and he has to stay inside."

Wordsworth and the Roast Beef Romance

I really wanted to tell her it wasn't necessary. Too bad there were other people in the kitchen.

Everyone finished breakfast and put their dishes in the sink. Dee Dee got my leash and clipped it to my collar.

"Okay, Wordsworth, let's go," she said, sliding open the kitchen door.

As soon as we were outside I dug in my paws. "We really don't have to go for a walk."

"Yes, we do," she said. "After all the roast beef you've had this week, if you don't get some exercise, you'll turn into a blimp."

"But it's windy," I said.

"So?"

"You know I don't like wind," I said. "It ruffles my fur."

"Come on, Wordsworth," Dee Dee said, giving the leash a tug. "Let's go."

I could see that she wasn't in a good mood. We started into the park. The leaves rustled in the trees and the wind blew Dee Dee's hair around.

"So you've really given up trying to help Roy?" I asked.

Dee Dee nodded sadly. "I thought I was helping, but I wasn't. I was only making things worse."

We reached the rocks and looked out at Bell Island Sound. The waves were big and tipped with whitecaps. They crashed against the rocks and sent white foam and sea spray flying into the air. But despite the bad weather, the sailboats were out racing.

"Don't they ever cancel the races because of the weather?" I asked.

"Not unless it's really, really bad," Dee Dee said. "Especially on the last day of Race Week. Everything ends today. They can't postpone it. . . . Look." She pointed toward a group of sailboats bobbing in the heavy seas. "That's the lasers. I hope Razel wins today."

Ruuuuumble . . . The sound of distant thunder grumbled through the air. The wind began to blow harder. Now the waves had bigger whitecaps.

"Uh-oh," Dee Dee said. "A storm is coming."

"Won't they stop the race now?" I asked.

"Not yet," Dee Dee said. "They'll keep racing until they see where the storm is going. It could pass to the north or south."

RUUUUUMMMBLE . . . The thunder was growing louder.

Crack! A bolt of lightning streaked down through the gray sky.

Ker-splash! The waves crashed against the rocks.

"Wow, I wouldn't want to be sailing today," I said.

CRASH! BOOM! The thunder sounded like an explosion. The waves were growing even bigger. Out on the sound, the sailboats were rocking back and forth like toys.

Split! Splat! Big drops of rain started to plummet out of the sky.

CRACK! The lightning was almost directly overhead.

Wordsworth and the Roast Beef Romance

The wind drove sheets of rain through the air. Dee Dee and I were getting soaked.

"I think we ought to go!" I said.

"No, look!" Dee Dee pointed at the sailboats. They were all scattered now by the storm. "They're being blown toward the rocks!"

Dee Dee was right. The winds were too strong. Many of the sailboats were being swept sideways toward the rocks on the shore of Bell Island Sound! We could see the kids in the boats struggling to steer away, but the winds were just too strong.

"Look, there's Razel!" Dee Dee pointed toward one of the sailboats. We could see Razel struggling to steer her boat away from the rocks. Dee Dee turned to me.

"This is really bad, Wordsworth," she said. "Run home as fast as you can and get Roy."

Twenty-four

***

I ran . . . then I stopped to catch my breath.

Then I ran some more. My tongue was hanging so far out that I almost tripped over it.

So maybe I wasn't in such great shape.

The trees were shaking wildly.

Crash! A branch smashed to the ground near me.

Finally I got to the house and went through the doggy door. I ran down the front hall and stopped.

The stairs loomed before me. I was panting hard. The last thing I wanted to do was climb steps.

But I had to. For Razel's sake.

I started up the steps. My legs were so tired they were trembling. I'd stopped panting and started wheezing. Finally I made it to the second floor.

Boom! Outside, thunder crashed.

I dragged myself down the upstairs hall to Roy's room. The door felt like it weighed a ton as I pushed it open. Inside, Roy was sitting on the corner of his bed, watching a game show on TV and lifting barbells.

Gr . . . oof . . . I couldn't catch my breath. I could hardly bark. Roy turned and looked at me.

"Wow, Wordsworth," he said. "You're soaked."

Arf . . . I was supposed to be barking excitedly. Like Lassie always did. I was supposed to get his attention and warn him of the danger. How come those dumb humans on TV always understand Lassie?

Roy kept lifting his weights.

Arf . . . It was no good. I was too out of breath to bark loudly. Roy wasn't even paying attention to me. In a few moments Razel and her boat were going to get smashed on the rocks!

Twenty-five

There was only one chance left. I staggered out of Roy's room and into Janine's. Janine's room was a mess, as usual. Softball jerseys hung on the bedpost. Various sneakers and athletic shoes were scattered around the floor, along with dirty socks. But I had only one goal in mind.

Her new telephone with her own line.

It was up on the night table. I took the cord in my mouth and yanked.

Clank! The telephone fell to the floor and the receiver rolled off. Very carefully, using my nose, I dialed the Chandlers' phone number.

Try dialing with your nose sometime. It isn't easy.

Out in the hall I heard the phone ringing.

Roy's door creaked open and he went into his parents' bedroom. I had to lie down on the floor and press my ear to the receiver.

"Hello?" Roy answered.

Wordsworth and the Roast Beef Romance

"Roy," I gasped. "Get down to the park fast. Some sailboats got caught in the storm. They're going to crash on the rocks."

"What?" Roy said. "Who is this?"

"A friend," I gasped. "Now hurry. Razel's in one of the boats."

"Who . . . ?"

Click. I pressed my paw down on the phone, disconnecting us.

A second later I heard Roy's footsteps in the hall. "Better go see what's going on," he muttered to himself as he headed down the stairs.

Bang! I heard the front door slam closed as Roy raced out into the rain.

Twenty-six

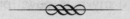

By the time I got back to the park, the rain was coming down so hard I could hardly see through it. The wind was whipping in my face. Some of the sailboats had managed to sail clear of the shore, but two were only a few dozen yards from the rocks now. The huge waves and fierce winds were pushing them closer.

I worked my way along the slippery rocks until I found Dee Dee. She was alone!

"Where's Roy?" I yelled as the wind made my ears flap.

Dee Dee pointed toward the sailboats.

I peered through the driving rain and saw him in the rough gray waters. Roy was actually trying to swim through the waves toward the closest sailboat!

"Is he crazy?" I yelled.

"Yes," Dee Dee yelled back. "But did you ever think he'd be so brave?"

"No," I said. "I just know that crazy and brave is a bad combination. People get hurt that way."

Roy reached the first sailboat. The boy sailing it helped pull him in. Together they managed to turn the sailboat around and steer it away from the rocks. That left only Razel's sailboat. Roy dove back into the water.

"My hero!" Dee Dee clasped her hands together. Her hair was plastered to her head. Her soaking-wet shirt clung to her skin.

Roy fought through the waves. He splashed toward Razel's boat. Waves curled over and crashed on top of him.

Razel waved her arms at him. "Go back, Roy!" she shouted.

But Roy kept splashing toward her.

Suddenly a big wave rose up and crashed right over him!

Roy disappeared in a swirl of white foam!

"Oh, no!" Dee Dee cried.

Twenty-seven

Had Roy drowned?

Razel peered desperately into the swirling waters.

"Roy!" she shouted.

A head popped up near the boat.

It was Roy!

He grabbed the gunwale and Razel helped pull him in. The boat was only a dozen yards from the rocks! Huge waves crashed against the rocks, sending spray into our faces.

"They'll never make it!" Dee Dee cried.

In the boat, Roy grabbed the ropes to the sail. Razel pushed on the tiller with all her might.

The boat was still being swept sideways toward the rocks!

"They're going to crash!" Dee Dee cried.

Twenty-eight

I hid my eyes with my paws. I couldn't bear to watch! The wind was howling. The rain washed down on me, soaking me to the skin. I waited to hear the crash of wood against rock.

And waited . . .

And waited.

"They did it!" Dee Dee suddenly shouted.

I took my paws away from my eyes. Somehow Razel and Roy had managed to turn the sailboat away from the rocks! They were slowly sailing through the waves back toward the harbor.

"Come on, Wordsworth!" Dee Dee yelled.

We started running along the wet rocks. Razel and Roy were sailing toward the yacht club. They were going to make it!

We reached the yacht club dock just as Roy and Razel sailed in. The storm had started to pass. The wind wasn't so strong and it wasn't raining so hard anymore. The dock was crowded with kids in life jackets. They were all talking about the storm. Dee Dee pushed through them and got to the end of the dock. Roy and Razel brought the sailboat in and tied it up. They were both soaking wet.

"Are you guys okay?" Dee Dee gasped, brushing the wet hair out of her eyes.

Roy and Razel looked at each other. Then they both nodded.

"Roy, I can't believe you!" Dee Dee cried. "You're a hero!"

"Shush." Roy pressed his finger to his lips. "Not so loud."

"Don't you want everyone to know?" Dee Dee asked.

Roy looked at Razel again. They both smiled. Then he turned back to his sister. "The only person who needs to know already does."

Twenty-nine

Race Week always ends with a big
party at the yacht club. Of course, dogs aren't allowed.

"You stay here, Wordsworth," Dee Dee said that
night. The storm had passed and the sky had cleared. It
was dark and we were on the front porch of the house.
Dee Dee had gotten dressed up for the party. Roy,
Janine, Flora, and Leyland had already gone down the
front steps and were waiting for her in the driveway.

"Can't I come?" I whispered.

"Come on, Dee Dee," Janine called. "Will you stop
talking to that dog already?"

"I'm coming," Dee Dee called back. Then she
turned to me again. "You can't come, but I promise
I'll bring you a treat."

Groof! I did the dumb-dog act. Dee Dee smiled
and kissed me on the head. Then she went down the
front steps and joined the others. They started walking
to the yacht club.

Wordsworth and the Roast Beef Romance

I waited until they disappeared around the corner. Dee Dee couldn't really expect me to wait there for her "treat," could she? Knowing how worried she was about my weight, she'd probably bring me a carrot stick or something.

As soon as the Chandlers were gone I headed for the yacht club. The smell of grilled shish kabob filled the air. I found that hole in the hedge again and went through. Once again I sneaked up behind the cooks at the grills. Large trays of uncooked kabobs lay behind them. All I had to do was—

"Ahem!" Someone cleared her throat behind me.

I turned. It was Dee Dee!

"Surprise, surprise," she said with a knowing smile.

"How'd you know I'd be here?" I asked.

"Just call it a dog owner's intuition," she said. "Come on, I want to show you something."

"Can't I have just one shish kabob?" I begged.

"Come on, Wordsworth," Dee Dee said.

She led me around the party and out to the dock.

"What are we doing here?" I asked.

"Shhh!" she whispered. "Look."

Two people were standing way down at the end of the dock. The moon was rising behind them. They were holding hands and facing each other.

"So?" I asked. "You dragged me out here to see that?"

"It's Roy and Razel," Dee Dee whispered.

113

"Huh?" I looked again. Dee Dee was right! In the moonlight, Roy and Razel moved closer to each other. Then their lips met.

"Isn't it romantic?" Dee Dee whispered, and rubbed my head. "Roy finally has a girlfriend."

"Yeah, great," I muttered. Then I turned around and headed back down the dock.

"Where are you going?" Dee Dee asked, catching up behind me.

"To get something to eat," I said.

"Oh, come on, Wordsworth, aren't you happy for them?" Dee Dee asked.

"I'm thrilled," I said. "Now where are those shish kabobs?"

Dee Dee started to follow. "Tell me the truth, is food all you can ever think about? Don't you ever think about love?"

I stopped for a moment and thought about it.

"Sure," I said.

"You do?" Dee Dee looked surprised.

"Yup," I said. "Sometimes I think about how I love *you*. But mostly I think about how much I love *food*."

"Oh, Wordsworth," Dee Dee sighed, and smiled. "You are too much."

Todd Strasser has written many award-wining novels for young and teenage readers. He speaks frequently at schools about the craft of writing and conducts writing workshops for young people. He lives with his wife, children, and dog in a place near the water.

KEEP YOUR EYES AND EARS—ON WORDSWORTH!

Wordsworth is a very smart talking Basset Hound and a member of a very strange family, the Chandlers. There's the utterly inept Mrs. Chandler, the bumbling Mr. Chandler, sixteen-year-old Janine—a pretty jock who'd rather play sports than date boys, fourteen-year-old uncoordinated Roy who would do just about *anything* for a date, and ten-year-old Dee Dee, wise beyond her years, who, together with clever Wordsworth, tries to keep the rest of the family out of trouble!

IT'S WORDSWORTH AND THE . . .
COLD CUT CATASTROPHE
KIBBLE KIDNAPPING
ROAST BEEF ROMANCE
MAIL-ORDER MEATLOAF MESS*
TASTY TREAT TRICK*   *coming soon

MONSTERKIDS

LOOK FOR THESE SPOOKY MONSTERKIDS STORIES BY GERTRUDE GRUESOME:

Drak's Slumber Party
Life isn't easy for a third-grader monster. Drak's just trying to fit in. That's why his slumber party has to be the best. But Drak's blood-sucking cousins have just arrived! Can he save his friends *and* the party?

Frank's Field Trip
Frank N. Stein has monster-sized problems. He can't seem to get a break—except when he's breaking things. His class is at the museum and about to lose the science competition. Everyone is counting on Frank to save the day!

Harry Goes to Camp
How will Harry Wolf survive a month of summer camp? Whenever there's a full moon, he needs to do what all werewolves do: eat raw hamburgers and howl at the moon. For Harry and his best friend Alec, will their first summer at sleepaway camp be a total disaster?

Boris Bigfoot's Big Feat*
He's the new kid in school, and he doesn't fit in. But when Boris Bigfoot starts kicking a soccer ball around, the coach sees his new star player. Before long, Boris not only fits in, he's the hero of the team.

The Curse of Cleo Patrick's Mummy*
According to ancient mummy legend grave misfortune will fall on anyone who dares to steal from a mummy. Cleo Patrick's mother can't find her favorite bracelet. Cleo and her friends play dress-up with her mom's jewelry, but they didn't steal anything. So why is everything going wrong?

Zelda's Zombie Dance*
Zelda LaMort has trouble making friends—it's hard to fit in when you're dead.

*coming soon